Clifford THE BIG RED DOG®

Picking Apples and Pumpkins

by Liz Mills

Illustrated by Tom LaPadula

Based on the Scholastic book series
"Clifford The Big Red Dog"
by Norman Bridwell

ISBN 0-439-73375-8

Designed by Michael Massen

10 9 8 7 6 5 4 3 2 1   06 07 08 09 10

Printed in the U.S.A.

First printing, September 2006

"Today is our field trip day," said Miss Carrington. "We will visit Farmer Brown's apple farm."

"I love field trips," said Charley.

"Clifford would love to visit a farm," said Emily Elizabeth.

Emily Elizabeth raised her hand.

"Miss Carrington," she asked,

"can Clifford come, too?"

"I don't see why not," replied Miss Carrington.

"Woof!" barked Clifford.

"Hooray!" said Emily Elizabeth.

"Let's go!" shouted the class.

"Welcome to my farm," said Farmer Brown.

"Shall we start with a hayride?"

"Yes!" shouted the class.
They ran to the hay wagon.

"I love hayrides!" said Jetta.

"I've never been on one before," said Charley.

"It's lots of fun," said Emily Elizabeth.

Farmer Brown turned the key
to start the tractor's engine.
Nothing happened.

Farmer Brown turned the key again.

The tractor still would not start.

"I'm sorry, kids," said Farmer Brown.

"My tractor is broken. It can't pull the wagon."

Emily Elizabeth had an idea.

"Clifford can pull the hay wagon!" she said.

"Woof!" barked Clifford.

Farmer Brown hooked Clifford up to the hay wagon.

It was not too heavy for the Big Red Dog!

Clifford pulled the wagon all around the farm.

Jetta waved to the cows.

Vaz waved to the pigs.

Emily Elizabeth waved to the ducks.

"This *is* fun!" said Charley.

Clifford stopped beside some apple trees.

"May we pick apples?"

asked Emily Elizabeth.

"Yes, you may," replied Farmer Brown.

Emily Elizabeth and Jetta
climbed onto Clifford's back.
They picked apples.
"Yum!" said Jetta.

Clifford pulled the wagon back to the barn.
The kids climbed out.

"Thank you, Clifford!" said Farmer Brown. "You saved the hayride!"

"Now it's time for arts and crafts," said
Miss Carrington. "We're going to make hand
turkeys."

Everyone ran to the picnic table.

On the table were cups of apple cider.

The kids traced the outlines of their hands on paper.

Miss Carrington helped cut out the outlines.

Then the kids decorated them to look like turkeys.

"Clifford, would you like to make
a paw turkey?" asked Emily Elizabeth.

"Woof!" barked Clifford.

Emily Elizabeth traced his paw on a big piece of paper.

She cut it out and colored it red.

"Perfect!" she said.

Then it was time to leave.

"Thank you for a great day,"

Miss Carrington said to Farmer Brown.

"Thank you, Farmer Brown!" said the class.

"You're welcome!" replied Farmer Brown. "Clifford, you can come work in my orchard anytime!"

On the bus, Miss Carrington asked,
"Class, what are you thankful for?"

Charley said, "I'm thankful for the hayride."

Jetta said, "I'm thankful for the yummy apples."

"I'm thankful for Clifford!"
said Emily Elizabeth.

"Woof!" barked Clifford.

Do You Remember?

Circle the right answer.

1. Who wanted Clifford to come along on the field trip?

   a. Jetta

   b. Emily Elizabeth

   c. Charley

2. How did Clifford help Farmer Brown?

   a. He ate all the apples.

   b. He took a nap.

   c. He pulled the hay wagon.

Which happened first?

Which happened next?

Which happened last?

Write a 1, 2, or 3 in the space after each sentence.

Emily Elizabeth made a paw turkey for Clifford. _____

Jetta waved to the cows. _____

Miss Carrington told the class they were going on a field trip. _____

Answers:

Miss Carrington told the class they were going on a field trip. (1)

Jetta waved to the cows. (2)

Emily Elizabeth made a paw turkey for Clifford. (3)

2. c

1. b